Glimpses of Life
Through Cobweb

Glimpses of Life Through Cobweb

Madhu N R

PARTRIDGE
A Penguin Random House Company

ISBN: Hardcover   978-1-4828-4572-3
           Softcover   978-1-4828-4571-6
           eBook   978-1-4828-4570-9

Print information available on the last page.

To order additional copies of this book, contact
Partridge India
000 800 10062 62
orders.india@partridgepublishing.com

www.partridgepublishing.com/india

Contents

To the soul of Jyothi, the brave tigress who fought with death for thirteen days before losing out.

Acknowledgements

I express my sincere thanks to Prof. Rajagopal who had painstakingly gone through the manuscript and suggested corrections. Rajagopal, sir, had taught me English during 1981–1983.

I thank Prof. Prasanta Purohit for suggesting the title of this book.

I thank Murali, my schoolmate who invited me to Facebook. I had started the blog www.madhucartoons. com for posting COBWEB which was simultaneously posted in Facebook also. When it was stopped after 365 postings, Murali asked me when the book was going to be released. It was Asha, another schoolmate of mine, who introduced me to Partridge. Another coincidence is that all three of us were schoolmates at St Joseph's Convent primary school (Quilon) from 1970 to 1975 till the fourth standard.

Preface

Man, the most intelligent fool, is the only creator of literary art. It is an irony that the same man manufactures weapons of mass destruction too.

Believers feel that God created man, and atheists say life originated in water. Both of them still have not proved their arguments. The Large Hadron Collider at CERN is also not going to give a definite answer.

Swami Vivekananda, who addressed Americans as sisters and brothers on 11 September 1893, was earlier an atheist, went to Ramakrishna Paramahamsa to make fun of him. When Narendra (Swami Vivekananda's earlier name) asked him whether he had seen God, the reply was, 'Yes, I can see him, more clearly than seeing you'. Narendra later became his most famous disciple. The world-renowned Swami Vivekananda later said, 'There is no god beyond universe.'

So what is God? The easiest answer is that God is within you and me. So where do we come from and where do we go to? Scientists say life takes shape in the mother's womb and the body perishes with death. It is as easy as eating a cake. But when we are alone, we are confronted by many questions regarding our identity. No answer consoles us. This book has nothing to do with God or religion.

I have heard that nothing fits into the pigeonhole, not even a pigeon. The writer is also like the pigeon. It is difficult for him or her to fit into the hole known as society.

Poems

Poems

Ode to a Tigress from India

Tears of Blood (16 December 2012 to 29 December 2012)

In a moving bus, on a chilly night
At Delhi, she was cruelly violated
Where cruelty, as a word, stands in shame
Even animals are ashamed of the six beasts
Nazi concentration camps are better off
Eight rapes, then by a rusty rod
Her intestines pulled out by a juvenile.
Why should she suffer?
Hearing her cries?
Pens go without words!
Even the wind stands still . . .
Let down by
Corrupt officers, insensitive politicians, helpless gods
For thirteen days, she fought like a tigress
With death
Then slowly succumbed to lifelessness.
In death also she saved India.
Had her life gone out in India
Delhi would have burned.

To save a chief minister's chair she was flown out.
Saving Delhi, saving politicians.
But the fire rages inside millions' hearts.
She was an Indian girl
But we couldn't save her honour and life.
Had she not the right to die in India?
Having gone, she is the only one
Not in pain.
Her only mistake was being born an Indian

A chief minister who was blown off in public ire
Booed!
Places a wreath in the middle of night
Unashamed!
Is she paying respects or
Adding fuel to the unseen rage
In many hearts?
Three surgeries on this
Little daughter of India.
'I want to live
Please save me . . .'
Hanging on to life
Her words make waves in the air
'Have they been caught?
Should be *burnt* alive . . .'
The wounded tigress whispered
In uncontrollable pain.
Her cries for help
Her wail of suffering, the inhuman torture
Drives an axe in your brain
You could go mad.
Had she been alive

Would have become India's icon
For the women of the world
Above Jhansi Rani.
Alas, we failed her!
Many corrupt and insensitive political fools
Have memorials in Delhi.
Where flowers pour and
Crocodiles come to mourn
At least twice a year
Where is her memorial, my countrymen?
The flames of rage burning in many hearts
Will come out and build a memorial for her
One day.
In the minutest of words, she is the
Joan of Arc of India.
And she will become Jyothi Ma (mother) to many
Giving blessings to a nation of helpless citizens.

A story from the wind
Far from Delhi, near to Bombay
In Pune
A youth goes to a home, of course
To rob.
The gold being fake
Enraged
Chops off the fingers of a sixty-five-year-old woman,
Follows with twenty-one stabs and kills her
Then rapes her pregnant granddaughter-in-law
And stabs her only nineteen times.
The young woman avoids her belly
Whilst taking the stabs to save her child.
Job done, the youth leaves
One mistake, the young woman was alive.

The youth given the noose
Goes to the Supreme Judiciary
Next only to God.
The mighty authority intervenes
And saves him from the noose
As he smelt alcohol then,
Hence can be reformed.
Also good conduct in jail saved his life
Kangaroos brought from Australia, in black coats
Surprisingly alcohol is not hanged(ok for 33 to 38)
Or the sellers booked
Given *swatanter* (freedom) from death.
Blame it on alcohol
After all,
This is only a story by the wind.

Aftermath
The ordinary people dread
The thought when
These six beasts may be declared as
Human beings by the supreme authorities
For after keen observation, they find out
That they walk on two legs
Like us!

Changing Seasons and Man

To escape a horrendous summer
Drive out and dive into the snows
To play with a snowman.
To escape winter
Ride a camel and go to a desert
To play with the dry sands.
Stay on for spring
To play with the chirping birds
And dancing flowers to the
Tune of a cool breeze.
Tell it to the birds
That you are changing to a bird or a
Migrating animal.
Swing from branch to branch
Like our supposed ancestors.
Erase the criminal spots on you
Join nature,
Be happy, and
Don't turn
Mother Earth to a
Killer.

Mother*

The core of a Carnatic raga
A lullaby
Which my mother forgot to sing or
Which I forgot as I grew up
Mother, the sweetest experience in life
The whole universe in a cradle
Swung gently by a mother . . .
A mother fights for her child till the last drop of life
A life which she willingly gives to her child.
The womb the safest place in the world
Very secure, where not even light pierces you.

*Already published in the book *A Sweating Mind*

Che Guevara!

Che Guevara
You have become a saleable commodity
To be marketed
Only by the anti-imperialists.
You spray revolutionary thoughts
Far and wide instantly.
Your picture
In which you stood in
Rage . . .
On seeing a boat full of arms
Being blown up
By counter-revolutionaries.
A pity even Ceauşescu
Displayed you
Before being shot to death by his
Own comrades.
The valour and rage against
Injustice, corruption, and nepotism
By the rulers.
Has it gone in vain?
Hijacked by neo-liberal revolutionaries
Who build castles with the sweat of the poor.

An Appeal

O goddess of justice
Remove your blindfold
Just for once
For the plaintiff
A hapless woman
Is dumb
Whom you cannot hear
But only see.

Shame, Shame, Puppy, Shame!

There were 4.9 ministers in our kitchen cabinet
All caught with their pants down
The whole state howled
Shame, shame, puppy, shame.
In our school days
We had lessons on morals
The subject called moral science.
The 4.9 ministers of the kitchen cabinet
Were inside the cupboards, with the skeletons,
Kept in the kitchen
Reading immoral science books
Shame, shame, puppy, shame.
As the energy sources of earth
Is depleting
Instead of conserving energy
These 4.9 ministers waste energy
Taking PhD on immoral science
And come to attend the kitchen cabinet
Exhausted, panting, and skinny
With hollow cheeks and protruding ribs
Shame, shame, puppy, shame!

The Absent-Minded Poet

The poet who went to inaugurate
a poetry session in a women's college
was given a sound thrashing
before being thrown out
for his verse began thus
'Spread your wings, not legs'.

American Politics

Two parties dominate American politics
Democratic Party and Republican Party
Followers of Democratic Party are Democrats
Republicans follow Republican Party
The Democrats are naturally anti Republican and
The Republicans anti Democrat
Hence literally the followers of both parties are against democracy
Which is a very sad state of affairs
For the oldest democracy
Fortunately in the literal sense
India doesn't have such mean thinking parties and
The largest democracy thrives.

A Day for Celebration

For avid newspaper readers
Is the day after
Holiday for the press
No news
No reading
No worries
Only happiness
And feeling good and
Free.

Jihad

Jihad is a shortcut to heaven for many
By mass killing of
Primarily Christians,
Secondarily Hindus, and
Lastly and unfortunately the poor
Muslims.

Who Wants a Father's Day?

None,
Not even the father,
All need the Mother's Day only,
Even the father doesn't remember his father,
But only his mother,
Hence abolish the Father's Day,
But doesn't the father need remembrance?
Time to save the fathers,
How about changing Mother's Day as Parents' Day?

Stories

An Idle Man in the Devil's Workshop

The Briton living near the forest was non-argumentative, unlike the Indian was, but restless for some days. He had no work to do. As he was an idle person, he had no entertaining daily routine like raising children, buying newspapers, milk, groceries, washing the clothes of his wife, etc.

Fed up with the world and himself, he left home and took himself across the river into the trees. The birds in the woods thought that he was for a morning stroll, and the bungling monkeys too didn't notice his red face filled with self-contempt and anger. The white man, who is the supreme creation of God, strayed deep and deep into the forest. It is obvious that only the white man, who is an intellect, was created by God. All other coloured men came out from the foolish and chattering monkeys, who do no work but only eat.

All the carnivores he came across were also idle like him. They were too lazy to prey on him. They were happy with their hunger, instead of working, like the poor African nations who are at war among themselves instead of doing agriculture.

At last he came to an abandoned bungalow. Fierce-looking nails were fixed on the compound wall and a running computer screen screamed 'Trespassers will be devoured', unlike the selfish giant of Oscar Wilde, who wrote that they would only be prosecuted. He went near the gate and saw the landlord's name hanging menacingly next to the gate: Satan.

As he was an ideal creation, he trespassed and went inside the bungalow. Satan was obviously a fool not to switch on electricity to the gate and wall. The Briton went to the supercomputer of Satan. Even though idle, he was a born computer expert who constantly ate meat from Buffalo instead of vegetable sandwich from Bangalore.

He began to change the settings of the computer. The screen on the compound wall now screamed 'Satan, get lost, now you have lost both heaven and earth'.

When Satan returned, he was shocked. As he touched the gate, he was thrown off by the high-voltage electricity. Satan gasped! He ran around the building yelling not being able to get inside.

As days went by, Satan could not bear the agony. He could not send hate arrows to the Middle East, Kashmir, or from North Korea to the South. The earth was becoming peaceful. Meanwhile some other terrible things also happened. In Burma, Aung San Suu Kyi was released,

Nobel Prize was given to the European Union signalling a no-war zone in medieval Europe, and to the horror of Satan, in India, inter-caste marriage increasingly got approved. Unbearable, Satan howled like a hungry wolf.

At last he decided to take the inevitable. He decided to meet his most hated enemy, the supreme power of the universe: of course, God. He appeared before God. He was ashamed of himself. There was no other alternative but suffer this. God looked at him gracefully.

'Well, Satan, have you changed?'

'No.' Unashamed, to get his way, Satan continued, 'I want help.'

God looked at him. 'You have turned the only living planet into your fiefdom—hell. What help do you want from me, my son?'

God's address was unbearable to Satan. The love coming in abundance from the gracious god pierced his rock-hard skin with a thousand nails. He quickly narrated his predicament.

God smiled. 'So you have been outwitted by a wily Briton.' God continued sadly, 'But there is a problem, a wily Briton can be outsmarted only by another wily Briton. Unfortunately, there are no living persons for this job now.'

'But, O God, what should I do? I was once your darling!'

God fell for it. He became sentimental.

'OK, Satan, there is a way out. There is a Briton named Ian Fleming. He tries to write spy stories. I shall give him a character named James Bond who loves only women and wine. He will help you. Bond will be given a license to kill and gamble. Go in peace, my child. Whosoever comes to me will return in peace.'

Satan disappeared instantly. It was like sitting on a throne full of thorns, to face the hateful, stupid, and generous God!

Satan waited for James Bond to happen.

Lord Rama's Dilemma

The celestial Rama sat with his head in his blue hands. Tomorrow is D-Day. Tomorrow I will kill the demon genius Ravana. The magnificent creature is to fall for one mistake perpetrated by a silly head.

Ravana was only a nine-headed genius, not ten as thought by many on the earth. The tenth head was his nemesis. It made Ravana steal his beloved Sita even though he intended to discard her later.

It is a pity that Ravana never saw reason. Hanuman's mission was also to advise him about this idiotic head. But Ravana didn't offer him even a stool to sit. More provocations led to the short-tempered Hanu burning half of Lanka.

The whole issue was created by Lord Brahma, a bitter rival of Lord Shiva whom Ravana adored. Ravana was created in such a form that even Rama couldn't find out the problem head. Had he known it then, everything would have been easy: just chop off that head. Even if the heads near to it would fall, Ravana will be left with some other heads. What a pity to vanquish such a multifaceted personality.

Now it was too late. Ravana would not listen to anyone. The problem was aggravated by earthlings also. They have a stupid belief that nothing can be stopped in its way: a thing bound to happen will happen! Rama saw in his inner eye a crescent-shaped arrow shot by him taking the neck of Ravana holding his nine good heads and one bad head, leaving the ugly headless body to fall.

My Eldest Sister's Youngest Daughter's Wedding

The title reminds you of Dostoyevsky's story 'My Uncle's Dream' (of a wedding). Unlike the readers of that story fainting midway or towards the end of the story, you will find my thoughts interesting, enterprising, and bound with traditions.

I am primarily a scientist with a doctorate, then an engineer, and finally a computer expert. The scientist's endeavour is with social science, politics, economics, astrophysics, astronomy, art, and on breaking social barriers, bombarding caste, wealth, and finally on organic foods for human beings' well-being and health.

Even though I am such a versatile genius, I am humble as a potato—the reason: first of all, I am an Indian and secondly, a South Indian.

I am now on a transatlantic flight over the Atlantic Ocean, second only to the vast Pacific Ocean. My destination is South India. I am to meet my tryst with destiny. Hope you understood my humble thoughts. Yes, friends, I am going to get married. To preserve the old culture and heritage values and customs of my remote metropolitan village, I am happy to announce that I am marrying my eldest sister's youngest daughter so as people, money, and faulty DNA don't go out of the family. From the airport, I have to catch the Chennai Express.

Dear friends, I am sharing my worries also. Someone had the affront to tell me that my sister and I are of the same generation and that her daughter is my daughter also. Who is going to heed to such brawling donkeys descended from foolish monkeys (with regards to the eminent scientist Mr Charles Darwin who propounded the theory that non-believers are blood relatives of an unknown primitive ape).

You are hereby warmly welcomed to my eldest sister's youngest daughter's wedding.

A Very Short Non-Sensual and Non-Sexual Story

It was the dead of night. One of the couple was having a 'hot' dream and woke up with an urge to copulate and woke up the other for a showdown.

Being woken up from the middle of a deep sleep, the other was not at all interested. Bored at the advances and cuddling and as the act was progressing at a high speed with dresses forsaken, the disinterested's brain woke up.

'Wait.'

The partner felt like a speeding car put to sudden brake, screeching.

'Why?'

'Show me your today's AIDS test report.'

The Curious Case of Prathap—an Associate Professor of English

This story is told by an approved sniffer. You may wonder whether dogs could tell a story. If dogs can bark, why not speak. After all, a dog is the favourite friend of man. You may say that man is not the favourite friend of dogs. The idea is stupid. The truth is that he is. Man invented the proverb 'Curiosity killed the cat that went to Mars' but never a dog even though dogs investigate many curious and suspicious cases. That is the passport to a dog's job as detective in Crime Bureau of Investigation of the World CBI(W).

This story is not a thriller but a dilemma. An associate professor draws a monthly salary of not less than 0.1 million rupees by which he can buy a Tata Nano car once in three months. But Prathap was not feeling happy. Some issues haunted him. But who is Prathap? Wait for the balance of the story.

Prathap was born, completed his studies, and works in Kollam, a town near Koyilandy near Kozhikode (previously known as Calicut), the land of the Zamorins. I sniffed through the case. Prathap works in a college run by the CCT (Casteless Community Trust), which of course takes a hefty sum as donation from aspirants for giving the job of lecturer in their colleges.

But Prathap's was not such a case. He never had to give money. Once the CCT members fought among themselves and the trust was taken over by the court for a brief period. It was at this time that Prathap got the job. He impressed the interview board and had to pay not a paise, save the rupee. But the whole world looks at him as a paid teacher. This was his dilemma.

These facts were found out by investigating a single line from one of Prathap's huge untitled poems. The line is 'How much will make the ship sink the sea into a desert'.

I felt terribly sorry for Prathap. But as a dog, what could I do but wag my tail happily when I see him. I became angry at the whole world which misunderstood my dear Prathap. I howled miserably—once for him and once against the world in protest.

Please don't take this seriously as paid teaching is the rule in garbage's own country. And as they say, barking dogs seldom bite and biting dogs seldom bark!

And the stupid story breaks off here.

Politicians (at Least) Cover Up Your Face!

The following event will never happen in India—which is a highly developed country with qualified politicians and satisfied subjects, with milk flowing as a white brook on one side of the road and honey flowing as a brown brook on the other. The citizens often get intoxicated with excess drinking of honey as a large quantity of sugar equals alcohol.

This somewhat devastating story happened in a location called BF (Burkina Faso) in the sub-African continent where nothing except starving people and thirsty animals existed. But as global economy prospered due to neo-liberal policies of different Marxist governments, BF also galloped. Money came in, and with it, democracy spread its wings.

Roads turned to runways and flights took off and so too politicians' ambition for wealth. Soon everything was done only with a commission, and the pack was led by the 10 per cent president.

When money came through unearned ways, politicians had to find a way to spend it. Soon sex became a hobby for them. They were supplied with girls in ice cream parlours and high ranges by loyal pimps. One even had the fancy in an airborne flight.

With the development of media, public consciousness also grew. Some sexual encounters of the fourth kind by them began to get exposed. People started questioning them. There was a voracious reader among the politicians in the ruling pack. He had read even the works of Vadakke Koottala Narayanankutty (VKN) hailing from a remote village called Thiruvilwamala in garbage's own country. The story told by the wise sexual politician runs like this.

The upper castes in a feudal village had the right to use any number of low-caste women for sex and have unlimited children in them. The children never knew that the landlord was their sperm donor. But one day, an urchin had the affront to call a landlord 'Dad!' The dad fumed and snorted, seeing that the lad left the land never to return.

People of BF were also beginning to behave like the undisciplined Keralite lad. 'What shall we do?' was the moot question. We have to continue with the commission, free sex, etc. But how?

They went to an old experienced journalist.

He advised, 'Use condom.'

'We use it, stupid.'

'No, you do not.'

'You want evidence?'

'You got me wrong. Use a big one to cover your face also.'

Thus the issue was settled and the whole scandal was covered up and the politicians lived happily ever after.

A Few Minutes with Dostoyevsky

It was a chilly night in St Petersburg. Dostoyevsky was in his living room, speaking with the characters of his novel *The Idiot*. Prince Myshkin, Nastasya, Rogozhin, Aglaia, Kolya, General Epanchin, and Totsky were in the room.

Suddenly a knock was heard. Dostoyevsky asked Kolya to open the door. Kolya came back with a bearded man. He looked familiar. *Where have I seen him?* wondered Dostoyevsky. He smiled at the stranger.

'Please come and sit. Kolya, a chair please.'

The man sat on the chair given by Kolya.

'May I know who you are?' Dostoyevsky asked him, smiling.

'I am Dostoyevsky,' the man replied.

The answer shook Dostoyevsky. To console himself, he laughed aloud looking at others. All of them smiled.

'I am Dostoyevsky,' he told the stranger firmly.

'I never said you are not Dostoyevsky,' he continued calmly. 'I am your conscience.'

Dostoyevsky was stunned. He had never faced such a situation before, not even in his imaginative world.

'I have come for a purpose,' the man said seriously.

'What is it?' Dostoyevsky was feeling irritated.

'I have come to fetch a person,' he said without any emotion.

All those in the room were terrified. They moved close to Dostoyevsky. The stranger continued.

'I came to take Nastasya Filippovna. She has mental disease and should be treated.'

'No,' Dostoyevsky said firmly. 'You may please go. I will not let anyone go.'

'Please don't be adamant,' the stranger said. 'I am saying this for the good of all. If she is treated, Rogozhin would marry her and Myshkin will marry Aglaia and all can live happily. Otherwise, the tragedy would be unbearable,' he warned.

Dostoyevsky stood up. He has had enough of this. His facial muscles tightened.

'No, never, it is not possible. I have completed the work.'

'Mr Dostoyevsky, please listen,' he pleaded. 'You should be kind to the emotions of the reader. You should not create tragedies on purpose.'

'Get out,' Dostoyevsky shouted.

Suddenly he fell down and had convulsions. He was having his routine fits. *It will pass over, nothing to be done,* thought the stranger.

The bearded stranger walked out with Nastasya.

Vincent Van Gogh Meets Death

Vincent Van Gogh was lying in the hospital bed. The room was dark. He could not distinguish whether it was morning or evening. The sleep that ended just now was full of bad dreams. Hounds chasing him and awakening suddenly, as he fell into a ditch. Such dreams have become a routine. Even when awake, he was having dreams that shook him. His favourite colour yellow never comes in these dreams. Yellow is a solace!

Suddenly he felt a severe pain. He was not sure what was causing it. Is this also a dream?

He saw someone beside his bed. A doctor or a nurse? The dress was white. The figure drew a chair from the corner of the room and sat on it near the bed.

Vincent saw that the figure was a man. He was holding something in his hand. It was a gun, and it was smoking!

Alarmed, Vincent asked, 'Who are you?'

The man smiled. He was extremely handsome with flowing thick black hair.

'Death,' the man replied calmly.

Vincent wasn't terrified. When he looked at the stranger, the pain became unbearable. Suddenly he understood what caused the pain.

'You shot me?' biting the pain, Vincent asked.

'Yes,' Death paused and continued, 'There should be a reason, Vincent.'

Vincent grew sad, his face wearing a dreary look.

'People will think I committed suicide.'

Death smiled, 'Does it make any difference?'

Yes, that would make no difference, thought Vincent. His was a wretched birth. No one understood him, his paintings, and his dreams, which were sweet earlier. Talent was a burden to him as it went unrecognized. Day by day he began to lose things—his sweet dreams, his talent for painting, and now he has lost himself. At times he couldn't even make out what he was or what was happening around him. Someone had brought him to this hospital for treatment.

'No, my friend, no,' he said sadly. 'That would not make any difference.' He fell silent for a while and continued, 'All these years, life was a torture for me. Now I am happy that it is going to end.'

Death was pleasantly surprised. This was the first time a man has addressed him as friend.

'Vincent, I am surprised. You are not afraid of me. People die mostly out of fear on seeing me.'

Vincent smiled. The pain was waning. He became weak and felt dizzy.

'I am not. I had more difficulties in dealing with your enemy.'

'My enemy, who is that?' Death was confused.

'Life.'

Death laughed and continued, 'What an irony, Vincent. All want life and run away from me. You are having casual talks with me.'

Vincent became curious of one thing. He asked, 'You are said to come in black attire. How is it that you are dressed in white?'

Death stared at Vincent gracefully.

'The actions of people make them see me as black or white. You have done not anything wrong, dear Vincent. I too am sorry that your life was wretched.'

A silence fell in between them.

'Vincent, I too can give boons. I give you an option. You can take all your paintings with you and return later as a painter once more or you can leave all your paintings here and return as an ordinary man. The choice is yours.'

Rebirth, Death was talking about rebirth, Vincent thought. Take all my paintings, my dreams, my treasure, and return once again as an artist. That would be great. Suddenly gloomy thoughts caught him. What if this disease comes with me then also, what if my life is wretched once more? Life would be repeating. No, not all artists are blessed with a good life. I can't bear this cross once more. He made up his mind and said firmly, 'No, Death. I will come with you barehanded. Let the paintings be here. I will return once more and enjoy these as an art lover or even buy it at a huge price.' Vincent laughed aloud. He felt light and happy. He was feeling so after a long time. Years back, he would feel elated for no reason, would be in high spirits for nothing, but lost it to his mental illness later. He felt like a bubbling baby in its mother's arms.

Vincent left his much mutilated body and followed Death like a lamb.

Introduction to Cobweb

COBWEB has two characters: one spider and a sloth. The spider is deadly poisonous and is waiting for a chance to catch the sloth when it falls on the web. The sloth, even though boringly slow, is wily. It never falls in the trap. These may be symbolic characters representing human beings.

The conversation is by two other characters in the form of question-answer or statement-counterstatement. One is Narayanan represented as 'N', and the other is Daridra Narayanan represented as 'DN'. Narayanan is another name of Lord Vishnu of Hindu mythology. Narayanan is a common name all over India. Some examples are N. R. Narayanamoorthy of Infosys Technologies, the famous writer R. K. Narayanan, etc. Daridra Narayanan was a term coined by the great Swami Vivekananda of India. Daridra means poor.

This is *NOT* - non-political, non-philosophical, non-sexual, non-satirical, non-ironical, and non-absurd.

Yours sincerely,
Madhu N. R.

COBWEB

Madhu N R

RANJAN MADHU

COBWEB 01
N: Like clay in the hands of the potter are we to God.
DN: That's old game. Like flies trapped in cobweb are you to the spider/fate.

⚬✗⚬

COBWEB 02
N: Is it safe to have extramarital affairs?
DN: Yes, provided your lover is from Mars.

⚬✗⚬

COBWEB 03
N: Is the minister in prison?
DN: No! Yes, sir, he is the minister of prisons.

⚬✗⚬

COBWEB 04
N: Some Italian food for thought: Is it Berlusconi or Berluscrewni?
DN: The former is a noun while the latter is a verb.

⚬✗⚬

COBWEB 05
N: Rain, rain, go away, come again another day.
DN: Yes, little Johnny wants to play indoor games.

⚬✗⚬

COBWEB 06
N: Is politics the scoundrel's last resort?
DN: No, it is his only resort.

COBWEB 07
N: Call Tom, Dick, and Harry.
DN: Impossible, all are ministers.

☯

COBWEB 08
N: What is a democracy?
DN: Where politicians are prosperous and give phosphorus
to citizens.

☯

COBWEB 09
N: Is a bank for women only to be opened soon?
DN: Keep your fingers crossed, the first two letters of
women may be deleted.

☯

COBWEB 10
N: Does the law permit you to commit suicide?
DN: No, but you are welcomed to get killed.

☯

COBWEB 11
N: Read the weather report.
DN: The climate is good, the weather is bad.
N: Then read the climate report.

☯

COBWEB 12
N: God has asked someone in Rome to stop work.
DN: I bothered Lord the least; stopped work voluntarily.

COBWEB 13
N: Where is Marie Antoinette now?
DN: In hell, eating her cakes.

ॐ

COBWEB 14
N: Does Shakespeare know English?
DN: I have a better question; does a fish know water?

ॐ

COBWEB 15
N: Is God alive?
DN: God is yet to be born.

ॐ

COBWEB 16
N: What is going on in China?
DN: Nothing to worry, Bo Xilai and his wife, Gu Kailai, are in jail.

ॐ

COBWEB 17
N: Can we create a colony like Great Britain?
DN: Yes, you can, with ants.

ॐ

COBWEB 18
N: Let the sun rise, let light prevail.
DN: Shut up, these things happen naturally.

COBWEB 19

N: Any difference between a cat and a tiger?

DN: Nothing significant that I have noticed yet.

∾

COBWEB 20

N: Did Great Britain love the subjects of her colony?

DN: Of course, as foxes love fowls.

∾

COBWEB 21

N: Mahatma Gandhi has said that a lawyer's profession is a liar's profession.

DN: What about the judges who also wears the same overcoat?

∾

COBWEB 22

N: Is God relevant today?

DN: Which god are you speaking of?

∾

COBWEB 23

N: How is it that the early bird always gets its worm?

DN: The stupid worm wakes up early and gets caught.

∾

COBWEB 24

N: What about the Indo-China face-off in North-Eastern Ladakh?

DN: They are facing farce since 1962.

COBWEB 25
N: The earliest worm gets up to be caught by the early
     bird.
DN: Better be late forever.

☙❧

COBWEB 26
N: Why are leopards so special?
DN: They do not know how to change their spots.

☙❧

COBWEB 27
N: Is your country God's own?
DN: Of course, garbage's also.

☙❧

COBWEB 28
N: Who is Steven Spielberg?
DN: Shh! He is an alien dressed as an earthling.

☙❧

COBWEB 29
N: What a pleasant day! What is the news?
DN: Shall I read the *Union Budget*?
N: Zzzz . . .

☙❧

COBWEB 30
N: Why is the goddess of justice blindfolded?
DN: To camouflage sleep.

COBWEB 31
N: After Fidel Castro, younger brother Raul takes over Cuba!
DN: Foul!

☙❧

COBWEB 32
N: When does God win?
DN: When the undefeated man dies.

☙❧

COBWEB 33
N: The difference between the genius and the mad?
DN: Both are possessed; one by good and the other by bad.

☙❧

COBWEB 34
N: Will the sun burn out one day?
DN: Don't worry, a substitute will be arranged.

☙❧

COBWEB 35
N: How is the visual treat in *Life of Pi*?
DN: $\pi = 22/7$

☙❧

COBWEB 36
N: Less luggage, more comfort.
DN: More money, less happiness.

COBWEB 37
N: Who was Brutus?
DN: Oh . . . only a close-friend slayer.

☙❧

COBWEB 38
N: Forget me not!
DN: Touch me not!

☙❧

COBWEB 39
N: Raja Harishchandra never lied.
DN: He never knew how to.

☙❧

COBWEB 40
N: I have a doctorate on bonobo chimpanzees.
DN: I have a doctorate on Vatsayana.

☙❧

COBWEB 41
N: A friend in need is a friend indeed.
DN: A Facebook friend runs away in crisis.

☙❧

COBWEB 42
N: What is a Facebook friend?
DN: Always 'hi' but 'bye' in need.

COBWEB 43
N: Is God real?
DN: Surreal, like the meerkats in *Life of Pi*.

ॐ

COBWEB 44
N: Does God exist?
DN: Yes, man doesn't.

ॐ

COBWEB 45
N: Man readily accepts God.
DN: A pity that God doesn't.

ॐ

COBWEB 46
N: The slogan of colony-time Great Britain?
DN: Find a land, build a nation, induct your government.

ॐ

COBWEB 47
N: Is life a maya?
DN: Very much. For example, there is no Mysore in Mysore pak.

(Mysore pak is a sweet.)

ॐ

COBWEB 48
N: The fortunate become rich, and the unfortunate become poor.
DN: That may not be true in philosophy.

COBWEB 49
N: Tell me about the growth of India post independence.
DN: Snails and sloths have won the race.

☙❧

COBWEB 50
N: Is $E = MC^2$?
DN: Hitler minus Einstein $= MC^2$.

☙❧

COBWEB 51
N: Lion is the king of animals.
DN: And the king is naked!

☙❧

COBWEB 52
N: Politicians treat us as donkeys.
DN: Treat them like donkey dung.

☙❧

COBWEB 53
N: Donkeys are ugly, lazy, and foolish creatures.
DN: Draw stripes on them; see the stunning zebra.

☙❧

COBWEB 54
N: The dumb never tell lies.
DN: The talkative newspaper tells only that.

COBWEB 55
N: Our country grows at 6 per cent.
DN: Corruption grows at 100 per cent.

∞

COBWEB 56
N: India's greatness lies in its ethnicity, traditions, and
    culture linked to a holy and conservative thinking.
DN: Conservatism is hypocrisy; travel in a bullock cart
    and say the above.

∞

COBWEB 57
N: Communism still rules China unlike Russia.
DN: The long wall protects them from neo-liberal
    capitalists.

∞

COBWEB 58
N: The central board of film certification needs a good
    chief.
DN: Appoint Tinto Brass, the Italian Vatsayana.

∞

COBWEB 59
N: Veg or non-veg—which is good?
DN: That depends—are you tiger or goat?

∞

COBWEB 60
N: Corporation budget is being passed.
DN: Or is it a corruption budget?

COBWEB 61
N: It is rumoured that Cleopatra had three breasts.
DN: But she had only two lovers.

⚬✕⚬

COBWEB 62
N: I want to see the god of your country.
DN: No problem, he is omnipresent and can be easily found in any garbage heap.

⚬✕⚬

COBWEB 63
N: For whom are the rules drafted?
DN: For common man, except judges and politicians.

⚬✕⚬

COBWEB 64
N: A lawyer's profession is a liar's profession.
DN: A judge's profession is hearing it.

⚬✕⚬

COBWEB 65
N: A woman was repeatedly raped by an auto driver, his friends, a policeman, his friends, and the whole community around them to cover up a mobile video recording of her bath.
DN: The anatomy of women being the same, they succumb to such things in God's own country and finally end the episode after revealing the ordeal to her husband.

⚬✕⚬

COBWEB 66
N: Difference between a fool and a politician?
DN: A politician always fools you while a fool always makes you feel wise.

COBWEB 67

N: Suppose in one room is your wife and in the other is
    your concubine, which one will you take?

DN: Oh god! I am between the devil and the deep sea.

☙❧

COBWEB 68

N: What does a critic see in a poem?

DN: Only some alphabets and words.

☙❧

COBWEB 69

N: Misunderstanding took the lives of Romeo and Juliet.

DN: Misunderstanding, thy name is Shakespeare.

☙❧

COBWEB 70

N: One day, India and Pakistan will reunite to become
    one nation.

DN: Yes, the day when the snake and mongoose become
    friends.

☙❧

COBWEB 71

N: At last, India has developed an underwater missile!

DN: We always spread our legs before sitting; the
    submarine will be ready in umpteen years.

☙❧

COBWEB 72

N: Is protection available by law?

DN: Take the easy way; get it from goons.

COBWEB 73
N: India exports even caste to England.
DN: A pity no foreign exchange is earned for it.

❧

COBWEB 74
N: Do you see a rival for Facebook?
DN: I see my nose . . . ah! It should be Nosebook.

❧

COBWEB 75
N: India and US to join in moon, Mars mission.
DN: I never thought that mission was a celestial body.

❧

COBWEB 76
N: The difference between dog and elephant?
DN: The dog's tooth and nails are sharp unlike the
    mammoth's.

❧

COBWEB 77
N: The extended version of the elephant's nose is its trunk.
DN: The extended version of the politicians' corrupt
    earnings is the Swiss bank.

❧

COBWEB 78
N: I feel like doing nothing.
DN: If you can't be the early bird, at least be the early
    worm.

COBWEB 79

N: The king is dead; long live the (new) king.

DN: The god is dead, long live the (new) god.

☙❦

COBWEB 80

N: Which is higher? Mount Everest or the heap of pending court cases?

DN: Want me to go to jail for contempt of court?

☙❦

COBWEB 81

N: Switzerland falls below ten in the list of least corrupt countries.

DN: The water in which they sail is mixed with others' corrupt earnings.

☙❦

COBWEB 82

N: What is one-way traffic?

DN: I can go, you cannot.

☙❦

COBWEB 83

N: If Octopus Paul predicted that Sociedad will win La Liga title?

DN: Hope Sociemom doesn't feel offended.

☙❦

COBWEB 84

N: What is the rule of the land?

DN: Life term for the accused, death penalty for the complainant.

COBWEB 85
N: My wife is an excellent cook.
DN: Which scripture says that women should cook?

⚬⚬⚬

COBWEB 86
N: Democracy is an excellent form of governance that survives all scars.
DN: The thick-skinned politicians never fear a scar.

⚬⚬⚬

COBWEB 87
N: India grows under the rule of efficient IAS officers.
DN: I thought it meant Inefficient Administrative Service.

⚬⚬⚬

COBWEB 88
N: There are only two Koreas, and they are at war.
DN: There are one thousand Indias in harmony.

⚬⚬⚬

COBWEB 89
N: Beating of hands and legs in water is swimming.
DN: The same sans water is life.

⚬⚬⚬

COBWEB 90
N: Tell me a contradiction.
DN: Not seeing reason is blindness with vision.

COBWEB 91
N: One bolt of lightning gives five billion joules of energy.
DN: Why not be clever to catch it and light up?

☙❧

COBWEB 92
N: Do aliens exist?
DN: They too have the same question.

☙❧

COBWEB 93
N: Politicians are solely responsible for our woes.
DN: We are for theirs.

☙❧

COBWEB 94
N: Margaret Thatcher was an iron lady.
DN: Would be difficult to decompose.

☙❧

COBWEB 95
N: Vatsayana wrote love stories with a feather, then called
    pen.
DN: Tinto Brass writes with a camera.

☙❧

COBWEB 96
N: Which flower should one offer his wife?
DN: The one that Nehru gave to Edwina.

COBWEB 97
N: What is acting?
DN: Nothing but controlling facial muscles.

∽

COBWEB 98
N: What is the job of the judicial department?
DN: To add pending cases.

∽

COBWEB 99
N: Rains play hide-and-seek.
DN: One day, they will play billiards.

∽

COBWEB 100
N: You are born to win.
DN: Win or lose, you will unfailingly die.

∽

COBWEB 101
N: India shifts to green, plastic banned!
DN: Corruption was also banned earlier!

∽

COBWEB 102
N: I intend to take a doctorate, give me a unique subject.
DN: Make a study on why people take doctorates.

COBWEB 103

N: It is sad that good friendships turn bad, see Caesar and Brutus.

DN: God was lucky to have been not killed by Satan.

৩৯

COBWEB 104

N: Is wife your best friend?

DN: Of course, hence don't befriend your friend's wife.

৩৯

COBWEB 105

N: Many animals and birds have become extinct; why not man?

DN: Because he has God.

৩৯

COBWEB 106

N: In our country, there are banks exclusively for criminals.

DN: Is it, meanwhile how is the weather in Switzerland?

৩৯

COBWEB 107

N: Sometimes I feel like a motherless child.

DN: Did your mother ever feel like a childless woman?

৩৯

COBWEB 108

N: Even though India is a developing country, her growth is sluggish as citizens are non-industrious.

DN: Exactly, no one has even bothered to write a second part to Kama Sutra.

COBWEB 109
N: Matthew Hayden says Sachin is India's Bradman.
DN: Truth indeed, but is Bradman Australia's Sachin?

ॐ

COBWEB 110
N: Sun is a paradox, burning forever.
DN: There was a beginning and there will be an end.

ॐ

COBWEB 111
N: Why doesn't God punish the corrupt?
DN: They take blessings from the god of corruption.

ॐ

COBWEB 112
N: Is it true that you marry the same person in all births.
DN: Hush! Don't let it out, man will lose interest in marriage.

ॐ

COBWEB 113
N: God proposes!
DN: Condom disposes!

ॐ

COBWEB 114
N: When do you feel to do only good things?
DN: When you go to hell.

COBWEB 115

N: British Parliament has two houses, Lords and Commons.

DN: Indian Parliament has also two houses, both are of Lords'.

ফ৶

COBWEB 116

N: The god you can feel?

DN: Electricity!

ফ৶

COBWEB 117

N: Difference between man and woman?

DN: Man needs sex; woman needs child.

ফ৶

COBWEB 118

N: What is the politicians' slogan?

DN: I will not trouble you if you do not trouble me without giving votes.

I will not trouble you if you do not trouble me with pestering questions after electing me.

ফ৶

COBWEB 119

N: Two unstoppable things?

DN: Ejaculation and death.

ফ৶

COBWEB 120

N: What is marriage?

DN: Two persons travelling in a boat which can carry only one and that cruises through shark-infested waters.

COBWEB 121
N: Animals hunt only for hunger.
DN: Man hunts only for pleasure.

☙❧

COBWEB 122
N: Contradictions of man in sex?
DN: Either he is a bonobo or a panda.

☙❧

COBWEB 123
N: Let's go to the film *Sex, Lies, and Videotape*.
DN: No need, read my autobiography.

☙❧

COBWEB 124
N: Why do you say sex has become a tragedy?
DN: Sex was conceptualized only for reproduction. The lazy
    rational man seeking everlasting entertainment made
    an art out of sex. He even documented chronicles like
    Kama Sutra and *Lady Chatterley's Lover* as guides. On
    the other hand, the irrational animals mate (they do
    not have sex) only during seasons. You should note
    that there are no rapes among animals.

COBWEB 125
N: Fire doesn't burn as it used to be!
DN: Water doesn't melt as it used to be!

☙❧

COBWEB 126
N: Heard? Bayern Munich vanquished Barcelona for 7–0.
DN: Caesar's solution was the best, offer each player a ball.

COBWEB 127
N: Difference between biography and autobiography?
DN: Latter is telling lies through your pen while the former is telling the same through others' pen.

૭૪૭

COBWEB 128
N: Criminals hate laws.
DN: Only fools love them.

૭૪૭

COBWEB 129
N: Why do you say women incapacitated India?
DN: Women gave birth to 1.2 billion idiots.

૭૪૭

COBWEB 130
N: 'Frailty, thy name is woman'—it is being said.
DN: 'Uncertainty, thy name is India'—it has been proved.

૭૪૭

COBWEB 131
N: Any similarity between laws and in-laws?
DN: Both are good in books.

૭૪૭

COBWEB 132
N: Difference between a leopard and black panther?
DN: The leopard reveals what the panther hides.

COBWEB 133
N: I intend to start a cartoon strip.
DN: Glad to hear, better than striptease.

ॐ

COBWEB 134
N: The greatest creation of God and man?
DN: Sperm and murder, respectively.

ॐ

COBWEB 135
N: Does future have a future?
DN: Yes, if past had a past.

ॐ

COBWEB 136
N: How does the sign of rupee look like now?
DN: Inefficient backbone lying comfortably in a cot.

ॐ

COBWEB 137
N: After suffering for centuries, man is asking God, 'Why
    did you create me?'
DN: God too is asking the same question.

ॐ

COBWEB 138
N: Man is an emperor in Europe with no death penalty.
DN: Magnanimous to let off even child killers (of James
    Bulger).

COBWEB 139

N: People join politics and become corrupt instead of becoming a statesman.

DN: No true statesman grew rich.

☙❧

COBWEB 140

N: While the politician's skin is thick, the lawyer's tongue is thick.

DN: Pity on the citizens and judges.

☙❧

COBWEB 141

N: Ignorance of law is not an excuse.

DN: Absence of law (in not hanging the juvenile killer of Jyothi) is also not an excuse.

☙❧

COBWEB 142

N: What about the future of man.

DN: Don't worry, man will continue as long as erections continue.

☙❧

COBWEB 143

N: The party has promised a stable government.

DN: Stable in corruption!

☙❧

COBWEB 144

N: The juvenile killer of Jyothi is not being hanged.

DN: This (killer) baby is being fondled by the judiciary, fed by the executive, and nurtured by the legislature to be released into the society where women are waiting to be raped and killed gruesomely.

COBWEB 145

N: A court has found that 'the alleged extramarital affair was not of such a nature as to drive the wife to commit suicide'.

DN: Thank God, at last such soft extramarital affairs are being legally approved.

❧

COBWEB 146

N: The new notion—being intimate with another woman, not cruelty to wife.

DN: Inti-*mating* equals cruelty to wife.

❧

COBWEB 147

N: Sad that Parliament conducts no business nowadays.

DN: The members have other good side businesses.

❧

COBWEB 148

N: The lawyer is an everlasting liar.

DN: He who speaks the most, lies the most.

❧

COBWEB 149

N: What about the Kennedy assassination?

DN: An accident, not assassination; Lee Harvey Oswald wanted to kill himself, and the shot misfired leading to a distorted history.

❧

COBWEB 150

N: If $E = MC^2$, isn't $MC^2 = E$?

DN: Smart indeed, meanwhile get me some milk from the Milky Way.

COBWEB 151

N: How is it that man, the only reasoning creature, doubts the existence of God?

DN: The creation has gone out of the Creator's hand; God never thought man would become so intelligent.

☙❧

COBWEB 152

N: One tells to go left, the other asks to go right, the third to go straight, and the fourth to go back. Whom should I listen to?

DN: Listen to others when asleep; listen to yourself when awake.

☙❧

COBWEB 153

N: Is wife your better half?

DN: Take care not to turn her into a bitter half.

☙❧

COBWEB 154

N: Tell a lie umpteen times and it will become true.

DN: Yes, as per our learned friends inside the court premises.

☙❧

COBWEB 155

N: There was a fire in the White House, and it is still smoking.

DN: Black or white?

☙❧

COBWEB 156

N: A cat has nine lives, a stitch in time saves nine; nine seems to be an important number.

DN: This is so because nine seems to be highest single digit number.

COBWEB 157

N: The minister has lost the election, analyze his present thoughts.

DN: For these five years, all I had made is a little black money.

☙❦☙

COBWEB 158

N: A wolf comes in sheep's clothing.

DN: Politicians in crocodile's.

☙❦☙

COBWEB 159

N: Silence is golden.

DN: It is also deafening.

☙❦☙

COBWEB 160

N: In the morning, a doctor thinks whom to treat, an engineer what to build, and a professor whom to teach; what does the politician think?

DN: From whom to take a bribe!

☙❦☙

COBWEB 161

N: To clear the confusion, shall I offer my head in a platter?

DN: No need, just resign.

☙❦☙

COBWEB 162

N: How are the politicians and the rhinoceros connected?

DN: Apart from the thick skin, both have no brains for good things.

COBWEB 163
N: What is the proof that man came out of monkeys?
DN: Both peel off the skin of bananas before eating it.

⚬

COBWEB 164
N: Polls are poles used by politicians to jump into power.
DN: Once in never out for generations.

⚬

COBWEB 165
N: The leopard's tongue is not bruised by its sharp teeth.
DN: The earth is not burned by the molten lava in its
    core.

⚬

COBWEB 166
N: When will India qualify for the football world cup?
DN: When each Indian player is allowed to use a ball and
    the Indian side does not have a goalpost.

COBWEB 167
N: Aim wins.
DN: Sincerity wins.

⚬

COBWEB 168
N: A lawyer always lies.
DN: Of course not, he does so only in the courts.

COBWEB 169
N: Who gets paid to tell and hear lies?
DN: Want to get me jailed for contempt of court?

∽

COBWEB 170
N: How should you close the computer?
DN: Shut up!

∽

COBWEB 171
N: Sex, lies, and videotape.
DN: In short, life.

∽

COBWEB 172
N: Tackle mice with cats and snakes with mongooses.
DN: Tackle life with determination.

∽

COBWEB 173
N: All enquiry commissions lack one page.
DN: Yes, the opinion of the common man.

∽

COBWEB 174
N: Is it a man's world or a woman's world?
DN: Both.

COBWEB 175

N: There may be light at the end of the tunnel, but this one is too long.

DN: Spread your nerves, and it will be six times the radius of earth. No tunnel is that long.

☙❧

COBWEB 176

N: Essentials of a good politician?

DN: Delivering blunders in public speech with the look of a genius and remaining confident of it.

☙❧

COBWEB 177

N: Swifts eat, sleep, and mate while flying.

DN: Such acrobatics are done by politicians too while in power.

☙❧

COBWEB 178

N: There are two different reports of the same incident in the same newspaper.

DN: Newspapers are meant to be read, not to be believed.

☙❧

COBWEB 179

N: Who cheats you the most in the land?

DN: Legislature, bureaucrats, judiciary, and paid newspapers.

☙❧

COBWEB 180

N: Prevalent diplomacy in South Asia?

DN: You cannot be friends with both India and Pakistan.

COBWEB 181

N: I testify to speak the truth, the whole truth, nothing but truth.

DN: Bored! Can't you sing Michael Jackson's 'Billy Jean' for a change?

ↂ

COBWEB 182

N: Even if the Indian side has no goalpost, we are not going to make it to the world football cup, but I am earnestly waiting for the day.

DN: It will surely happen on the day a deer kills a tiger.

ↂ

COBWEB 183

N: Strike while the iron is hot and make hay while the sun shines.

DN: Proverbs were invented to suit man's convenience; one that is not said but often done is 'Rob when the house is open'.

ↂ

COBWEB 184

N: We know of man's attitude to woman as a sex object, what about women?

DN: Refer to the criticism written by Sage Vatsayana's wife on his one and only masterpiece.

ↂ

COBWEB 185

N: What about the judiciary of your land?

DN: It is an old fallen elephant trying to get up.

COBWEB 186

N: The new CJU (Chief Justice of Utopia) has demanded a fixed term of two years for his job.

DN: Very good as he is sincere to bring down the pending cases, but there should be a rider that in case the pending cases are not eliminated, he shall be hanged/imprisoned till death.

⨯

COBWEB 187

N: The outgoing CJU (Chief Justice of Utopia) has demanded an apology from the incumbent CJU.

DN: Ask him to send a solicitor's notice and then file a petition in the trial court and to be pursued in high and super courts. A final decision will be awarded definitely in 150 years or his third, rebirth whichever is later.

⨯

COBWEB 188

N: Vatsayana was sidelined during his time.

DN: Should have made him the cabinet rank minister of sexual affairs.

⨯

COBWEB 189

N: Monkey or ma ki, which is racial abuse?

DN: Shut up, the baby-faced cricketing genius has given the answer.

⨯

COBWEB 190

N: Moon gets its light from the sun, yet poems are written about the moon leaving out the sun.

DN: Sun pierces the eyes of the poet while moon pierces his heart.

COBWEB 191

N: Gandhiji has said that untouchability is a crime against God and man.

DN: Saving a racist abuser is back-stabbing humanity (with reference to monkeygate).

സ

COBWEB 192

N: Why were women created attractive?

DN: Another blunder of God. He thought that man, like the panda, would become uninterested in sex and humanity would cease.

സ

COBWEB 193

N: Is ma ki an evolution of monkey?

DN: Sachin Tendulkar says so.

സ

COBWEB 194

N:What about population explosion?

DN: Book your ticket to Mars urgently.

സ

COBWEB 195

N: Sachin and Messi are geniuses.

DN: True, but Sachin lacks the power of Lara, and Messi, Maradona's appearance.

സ

COBWEB 196

N: When do we lose our innocence?

DN: When we begin to think.

COBWEB 197

N: Harbhajan Singh is a lion.

DN: Indeed, lions never call other beings monkey; the monkeygate scandal is absolutely false like the non-existent full moon light.

❦

COBWEB 198

N: Hardcore criminals in your land are spared the noose.

DN: Chicken-hearted judges who fear that the zombie of the hanged convict will be in his bedroom is not fit to be in that seat.

❦

COBWEB 199

N: I suspect a lawyer's brain in twisting the monkey into 'ma ki'.

DN: So what! Ma ki is running in full house in the literary circles of English-speaking cricketing nations.

❦

COBWEB 200

N: Cobweb is 200 today.

DN: The spider has miles to go before the sloth sleeps (with apologies to Robert Frost).

❦

COBWEB 201

N: The monkeygate?

DN: Sachin has unknowingly created a mutant monkey that is going to haunt him for life.

❦

COBWEB 202

N: What do courts do?

DN: Allow objections and adjournments.

COBWEB 203

N: Is Sachin's retirement early or belated?

DN: Hmm . . . let's see, if he had got the 100 centuries and 200 tests ten years ago, he would have been doing other businesses now.

☙❧

COBWEB 204

N: The *Hindu* daily has brought back its family members to the management as well as the editorial board.

DN: That shows all divine businesses like newspapers and politics are family oriented.

☙❧

COBWEB 205

N: Sachin retires on his 200th test.

DN: Life is only beginning for him; the sports minister has invited him for a big role in the ministry, already an MP, maybe next would be Bollywood or even Hollywood.

☙❧

COBWEB 206

N: The news channels are showing the same news repeatedly for hours.

DN: That is the only way to get things into the stupid heads of the viewers.

☙❧

COBWEB 207

N: For all his records, Sachin should be forgiven for his only mistake 'ma ki' and we should move on.

DN: But invoking mother to cover a crime is unpardonable.

COBWEB 208

N: The *Times of India* reports that Sachin holds sixty-nine records.

DN: VAT 69!

ஓஸ்

COBWEB 209

N: *Times of India* (14/11/2013) has published the photo of the monkeygate hearing held in Adelaide.

DN: In the photo, the body language of Harbhajan Singh clearly shows that he is the culprit and he is also confident that (the cricket) God (Sachin) will come to his rescue.

ஓஸ்

COBWEB 210

N: A pity that Sachin retires.

DN: A pity that Sachin didn't bite the bait of staying for some more years to score 200 centuries, 400 test matches, and 100,000 runs.

ஓஸ்

COBWEB 211

N: Everyone wants Sachin to be appointed as the sports minister!

DN: Then what would the current sports minister (Jitendra Singh) do, play cricket?

ஓஸ்

COBWEB 212

N: At last the truth is out, Mukesh Ambani says that chicken came first (even before eggs) in answer to KFC.

DN: Even before God?

COBWEB 213

N: The higher court has asked not to rush the appeal of death penalty given to Jyothi's killers.

DN: The defence lawyers wanted time, and they got it. The translations could have been done daily earlier itself if proper questions were addressed at the beginning of trial (those who are arguing and hearing are present or past lawyers who clearly know the methods of prolonging a trial). When the translations come, the convicts may appeal that they are illiterate and be allowed time to study the language to read it.

ന്ദ

COBWEB 214

N: My neighbour says that Cleopatra comes every night to his pool for a swim.

DN: Cleopatra is the name of his dog.

ന്ദ

COBWEB 215

N: Which sports has the highest fan base?

DN: Sex.

ന്ദ

COBWEB 216

N: We have occupied Wall Street, what next?

DN: Mars.

ന്ദ

COBWEB 217

N: Why should you never give the microphone to a writer?

DN: Revolutions start through speech.

COBWEB 218

N: A rapist is enjoying life to the hilt and your judiciary lets him off for frivolous reasons or sends him to a moral correction class.

DN: The darkest places in hell are reserved for those who maintain their neutrality in times of moral crisis (Dante in 'Inferno', *Divine Comedy*).

☙❧

COBWEB 219

N: The British cultured the aboriginals by establishing colonies.

DN: They not only looted and made interracial generations but also spread English language.

☙❧

COBWEB 220

N: Shall I read Kama Sutra?

DN: At your own peril.

☙❧

COBWEB 221

N: Why do you say Great Britain was a nation killer?

DN: The British came to South Asia's land mass, then called India, a peninsula of 600 princely states who united only to oust them. If they had not come, the world would have got 600 more nations with 'honest' and 'efficient' leaders.

☙❧

COBWEB 222

N: Sky should be the limit for our ambitions.

DN: The non-existent sky is a blue lie.

☙❧

COBWEB 223
N: Is D. H. Lawrence the Vatsyayana of England?
DN: Lady Chatterley's.

❦

COBWEB 224
N: A seventy-five-year-old person sleeps for twenty-five
   years!
DN: Sleep is the stepping stone to success.

❦

COBWEB 225
N: What is the alternative to bad politics?
DN: Democracy evolved out of monarchy but became
   bad; alternatives are yet to be evolved/invented.

❦

COBWEB 226
N: Statesmen have no realm to function unlike politicians
   who have politics.
DN: Why do we get more politicians and less statesmen?

❦

COBWEB 227
N: Should we celebrate life?
DN: Certainly, but without money.

❦

COBWEB 228
N: What is the cause of wars?
DN: Blind patriotism.

COBWEB 229

N: What is the politicians' call on development in your
    land?

DN: On your mark, get set, don't go!

ॐ

COBWEB 230

N: Einstein has said that God does not play dice.

DN: Nor steal, but politicians do both.

ॐ

COBWEB 231

N: This is an era of coalition politics.

DN: And of allied corruption.

ॐ

COBWEB 232

N: The British prime minister lives in Downing Street.

DN: Downing equals waning equals thinning, no wonder
    the sun of the British Empire set, never to rise again.

ॐ

COBWEB 233

N: Your PM lives in Race Course Road.

DN: And the country gallops.

ॐ

COBWEB 234

N: What if lightning brought gold?

DN: It brings; to take it, you should go to heaven.

COBWEB 235
N: What do politicians fear most these days?
DN: Will someone hack the password of his Swiss bank
    account.

☙❧

COBWEB 236
N: My mind is as clear as the blue sky.
DN: Both are not an insurance against prospective storms.

☙❧

COBWEB 237
N: Is autobiography fiction?
DN: Yes, for the author.

☙❧

COBWEB 238
N: Your hairline is thinning.
DN: Easier to scratch the head.

☙❧

COBWEB 239
N: What if the barber asks you to take the hair also?
DN: Better be bald.

☙❧

COBWEB 240
N: Duryodhana hated only the Pandavas.
DN: Hitler hated only the Jews.

☙❧

COBWEB 241

N: India celebrates girls attaining puberty.

DN: Why are boys' attainment of sperm not celebrated?

❧

COBWEB 242

N: Oh my god! See the giant strides made by the feminists.

DN: There, you too are an anti-feminist. Say 'Oh my goddess!'

❧

COBWEB 243

N: No country respects women as India does.

DN: Yes, here women are raped with their consent.

❧

COBWEB 244

N: Khap panchayats are necessary for preserving our age-old traditions and culture.

DN: For preserving votes also.

❧

COBWEB 245

N: Why do women grow long hair?

DN: Feminism begins from hair.

❧

COBWEB 246

N: Water sustains life.

DN: Thank God fishes have gills lest they would have drunk all the oceans.

COBWEB 247
N: I have a dream.
DN: Good or bad?

∾

COBWEB 248
N: What is most outrageous?
DN: Beating up of men and raping women.

∾

COBWEB 249
N: Who/what is (a) genius?
DN: Genius is one who can watch him/herself.

∾

COBWEB 250
N: The cause of World War II?
DN: German nationalism—of, for, and by the Germans only.

∾

COBWEB 251
N: Is there a law for ethics?
DN: Yes, even though it is unwritten, you are bound to follow it.

∾

COBWEB 252
N: I have a dream.
DN: Nothing wrong as you always sleep.

∾

COBWEB 253
N: Happy New Year!
DN: New Year and complimenting each other are routine affairs.

❧

COBWEB 254
N: Is Superman a super genius?
DN: Genius is associated with earthlings only.

❧

COBWEB 255
N: Overconsumption of alcohol leads to immorality.
DN: Underconsumption leads to underdevelopment.

❧

COBWEB 256
N: Life is so monotonous—same people, same place, same food—what a bore!
DN: The solution is in maths—minus x minus = plus.

❧

COBWEB 257
N: What is the contradiction of the day?
DN: All lawyers are liars, but all liars are not lawyers.

❧

COBWEB 258
N: A beggar refused the coin I offered him.
DN: Henceforth offer him bitcoin

COBWEB 259
N: Charlie Chaplin's mother went insane due to poverty.
DN: The clown was crying inside when you were laughing
    at him.

∞

COBWEB 260
N: Time stops for none.
DN: What stops for whom?

∞

COBWEB 261
N: What is unlimited tolerance known as?
DN: Mother.

∞

COBWEB 262
N: Tell me another contradiction.
DN: A remote and primitive South Asian state has two
    prime ministers, one official and another unofficial.

∞

COBWEB 263
N: When will Godot arrive?
DN: Some say he has arrived with a broom in Delhi.

∞

COBWEB 264
D: These days, newspapers have a lot of advertisements.
DN: But you don't have to pay for it.

COBWEB 265
N: Newspapers are the strongest pillar of a democracy.
DN: Wrong, *paid* newspapers are.

☙❧

COBWEB 266
N: The PM is in town.
DN: Better stay at home for it is safer for him and you.

☙❧

COBWEB 267
N: Are there bullet trains in your land?
DN: No, but we do have bullets.

☙❧

COBWEB 268
N: The bane of your land's democracy?
DN: We cannot call back the corrupt legislators once we have elected them.

☙❧

COBWEB 269
N: Two hours in the gym allows you to take all your favourite foods.
DN: Quick, arrange a bed for me at the gym.

☙❧

COBWEB 270
N: How can depression be cured without medicine?
DN: Proper exercise, proper sunlight, and proper food keep depression away.

COBWEB 271
N: Have you taken the one-way ticket to Mars?
DN: No, as long as they are not offering the return ticket.

ⓔⓧⓞ

COBWEB 272
N: I do things in such a way that causes minimum discomfort for others.
DN: Good, but how about your political leaders?

ⓔⓧⓞ

COBWEB 273
N: Everyone wants to be white.
DN: Snow melts at the first sunshine unlike rock.

ⓔⓧⓞ

COBWEB 274
N: Doctors too say that apple is a medicine.
DN: Eat this medicine with its cover.

ⓔⓧⓞ

COBWEB 275
N: White, black, yellow, and brown—man comes in different colours.
DN: Blood and revolution comes only in one colour.

ⓔⓧⓞ

COBWEB 276
N: The other side of midnight?
DN: Mid noon . . . on the other side of the globe.

COBWEB 277
N: Tell me an unrecorded postscript.
DN: Kama Sutra should have had a warning: 'Author is
 an unqualified sexologist, views are personal.'

☙❧

COBWEB 278
N: Does money open all doors?
DN: Yes, even heaven's.

☙❧

COBWEB 279
N: Why do politicians feel elated on winning an election?
DN: For being at your service, sir!

☙❧

COBWEB 280
N: I am respected by sycophants.
DN: Never respect a sycophant.

☙❧

COBWEB 281
N: When does the saddest part of a loan begin?
DN: When the repayment begins.

☙❧

COBWEB 282
N: Heard the president's Republic Day speech?
DN: Rubber stamp turned to iron!

COBWEB 283
D: A bloodless revolution is happening in Delhi.
DN: Let us hope it doesn't go as fast as it came.

૭૪૭

COBWEB 284
N: Your view of loans?
DN: Loans, like life, take out energy as it grows old.

૭૪૭

COBWEB 285
N: Your supreme court has disallowed the review on Sec.
    377 (Homosexuals and Lesbians).
DN: Justice is being buried in the chambers of judges.

૭૪૭

COBWEB 286
N: Your view on beauty?
DN: Never let your beauty spoil your life.

૭૪૭

COBWEB 287
N: One of VKN's stories ends as 'I died, I buried myself'.
DN: If he was not properly recognized during his lifetime,
    the people of his land should do so.

(VKN is a Malayalam satire writer.)

૭૪૭

COBWEB 288
N: Are loans without interest available?
DN: Yes, when they are undistributed.

COBWEB 289
N: Is there honey on the moon?
DN: No, you have to make it on earth.

☙

COBWEB 290
N: Any New Year's resolution?
DN: 365, none to be implemented.

☙

COBWEB 291
N: Should we respect others, or should we be sycophants?
DN: Be respectable.

☙

COBWEB 292
N: No one pays to go to hell.
DN: The game changes if hell is manned by women.

☙

COBWEB 293
N: Difference between man and animals?
DN: One needs clothes while the other doesn't.

☙

COBWEB 294
N: Is India a free country?
DN: I do not know; Poornam Viswanathan* said it first.

*Poornam Viswanathan (stage and movie actor) first
    announced it in All India Radio.

COBWEB 295
N: Is *War and Peace* a boring classic?
DN: Tolstoy must have written it in his sleep.

❧

COBWEB 296
N: Richard Nixon called Indians natives.
DN: White natives versus brown natives.

❧

COBWEB 297
N: Tell me an irony.
DN: People crave for a wet summer and a warm winter.

❧

COBWEB 298
N: Unlike in a drama, you can see explosions in a movie.
DN: You can feel (read) it in a drama.

❧

COBWEB 299
N: Do you get pesky calls from Swiss banks?
DN: Only people who are born to serve people are eligible
    for it.

❧

COBWEB 300
N: Why has Godot not arrived yet?
DN: Unavailability of return ticket?

COBWEB 301

N: Lokamanya Tilak said, '*Swaraj* is my birthright'.

DN: For present-day politicians, it is corruption.

⚬✕⚬

COBWEB 302

N: Is your land a democracy?

DN: Yes, but of, by, and for the criminals.

⚬✕⚬

COBWEB 303

N: When you say 'Good morning' in the East, it is 'Good night' in the West.

DN: One death leads to another birth.

⚬✕⚬

COBWEB 304

N: MGR and M. N. Nambiar were friends in real life.

DN: They were paid to be enemies on screen.

⚬✕⚬

COBWEB 305

N: What is the court's policy?

DN: Crime without evidence is not recognized.

⚬✕⚬

COBWEB 306

N: Women are good at screaming.

DN: Men are good at making them.

COBWEB 307
N: Rain or shine, you have to walk.
DN: Walk the talk.

ॐ

COBWEB 308
N: Idols bear feet of clay.
DN: Then worship only clay idols.

ॐ

COBWEB 309
N: It is said that politics is the last resort of scoundrels.
DN: Only resort.

ॐ

COBWEB 310
N: Elephants are revered in Kerala as they have Lord
    Vinayaka's head.
DN: Lord Vinayaka has an elephant's head, but elephants
    do not have Lord Vinayaka's head.

ॐ

COBWEB 311
N: Is your father an autocrat?
DN: Not in front of my mother.

ॐ

COBWEB 312
N: A book named *In Spite of the Gods: The Rise of Modern
    India* is out.
DN: Should have been *In Spite of the Politicians.*

ॐ

COBWEB 313

N: There are 702 domesticated elephants in Kerala.

DN: Keralites are infatuated by big things.

ⓧ

COBWEB 314

N: Tolstoy's *War and Peace* contains 560,000 words.

DN: The Nobel that the writer missed should be given to the one who counted.

ⓧ

COBWEB 315

N: What are fast track courts?

DN: Courts that give verdict even before filing of petitions.

ⓧ

COBWEB 316

N: Should Western Ghats be protected?

DN: If water is not an essential item, the answer is *no*.

ⓧ

COBWEB 317

N: Courts slumber till they get clinching evidence for a conviction.

DN: Law should compel criminals to drop evidence in each crime scene.

ⓧ

COBWEB 318

N: Why are judges given immunity?

DN: To give the verdict they like.

COBWEB 319
N: A bird in hand is worth two in the bush.
DN: Going by the pace of destruction of nature, neither the bird nor the bush will be there in the future.

☙❧

COBWEB 320
N: Saw a fast track court today.
DN: Is the track wide enough for the judges, lawyers, and litigants to run.

☙❧

COBWEB 321
N: Don't judge a book by its cover.
DN: Any harm in judging the cover?

☙❧

COBWEB 322
N: Frankenstein killed its creator.
DN: Man is doing the same to nature.

☙❧

COBWEB 323
D: I love school but hate studies.
DN: That's bad; either you should hate both or love both.

☙❧

COBWEB 324
N: Is Kerala developed, developing, or underdeveloped?
DN: Underdeveloped in roads, developing in IT, and developed in alcohol consumption.

COBWEB 325
N: Should man protect nature?
DN: Look at the irony: nature created man and pleads to
   him for protection.

☙❧

COBWEB 326
N: What are the good, bad, and ugly things in life?
DN: Love is good, money is bad, and hate is ugly.

☙❧

COBWEB 327
N: Life is a drama.
DN: Dream is a movie.

☙❧

COBWEB 328
N: Justice delayed is justice buried for the plaintiff.
DN: The more the delay, the better for the accused/killers.

☙❧

COBWEB 329
N: Your land doesn't allow non-procreational sex (Sec. 377).
DN: Yes, only recreational sex is allowed (rape in public
   view).

☙❧

COBWEB 330
N: Most yesteryear king(s) today have no palace, kingdom,
   or wealth.
DN: Same is the case for (par)king also.

COBWEB 331

N: What if some lawyer convinces a judge that the earth is flat?

DN: Get ready to be flattened by the judgement.

☙❧

COBWEB 332

N: Fed up with being late forever and saying sorry.

DN: Incompetence, thy name is sorry.

☙❧

COBWEB 333

N: In rain, trains run in tears.

DN: Charlie Chaplin too liked to walk in rain to hide his tears.

☙❧

COBWEB 334

N: Crimea has had a referendum.

DN: Ill timed! It should have been after the annexation.

☙❧

COBWEB 335

N: I am afraid to look at the trousers of Robert Pattinson. It may slip down any minute!

DN: Solved all your other problems?

☙❧

COBWEB 336

N: India punches in the nose of Sri Lanka from Tamil Nadu and sides with Japan in building ports in the island.

DN: Running with the hares and hunting with the hounds.

COBWEB 337
N: Kerala is God's own country.
DN: Here even God uses alcohol.

☙❦❧

COBWEB 338
N: 'Let truth prevail' is the motto.
DN: 'Let injustice prevail' is the fact.

☙❦❧

COBWEB 339
N: The thin line that separates journalism and creative writing?
DN: Truth.

☙❦❧

COBWEB 340
N: Egypt is the gift of Nile.
DN: Kerala is the gift of alcohol.

☙❦❧

COBWEB 341
N: Why don't animals need exercise?
DN: As they have no sense.

☙❦❧

COBWEB 342
N: Is Large Hadron Collider of any use?
DN: No, as any question regarding the hen or egg, which came first, will remain unanswered.

COBWEB 343
N: What is the importance of April Fool's Day?
DN: It is the day the Indian financial year starts.

❦

COBWEB 344
N: General elections are the killing fields of politicians.
DN: It is the only time the guns of the public work.

❦

COBWEB 345
N: L. K. Advani wants to be the PM.
DN: Give him a walking stick to race to 7 Race Course
    Road, New Delhi.

❦

COBWEB 346
N: Why do we love Mickey Mouse?
DN: As he is not a rat.

❦

COBWEB 347
N: What value does a woman give to tears?
DN: Zero.

❦

COBWEB 348
N: Are Asians still a burden to the white man?
DN: With reference to Afghanistan and the Middle East,
    yes.

❦

COBWEB 349
N: The difference between a thief and a bandit?
DN: The bandit is empowered to rob the thief.

☯

COBWEB 350
N: Why are animals naked?
DN: Their gods are naked.

☯

COBWEB 351
N: Does the whole of Indian Ocean belong to India?
DN: Yes, go and live with the fishes.

☯

COBWEB 352
N: Why the name Moody's (Investors Service)?
DN: Financial forecasts are always moody.

☯

COBWEB 353
N: The two great boxers who never fought?
DN: Muhammad Ali and Cassius Clay.

☯

COBWEB 354
N: Tell me two rhyming words having the same meaning.
DN: Society and brutality.

COBWEB 355
N: Tell something about cucumber and cumbersome.
DN: Cucumber some.

ೢಝ

COBWEB 356
N: Oral observation of judges has no value in law.
DN: Talk less, write more (verdicts).

ೢಝ

COBWEB 357
N: MT* has said that literature is only about love and
    money.
DN: Literature thrives as man's want for both never
    diminishes.

*M. T. Vasudevan Nair is a writer in Malayalam and is
    the Jnanpith Award winner of 1995.

ೢಝ

COBWEB 358
N: Do butterflies fear rains?
DN: No, as the leaves protect them from the unruly
    waters.

ೢಝ

COBWEB 359
N: The sentence banned even in hell?
DN: Heil Hitler.

ೢಝ

COBWEB 360
N: Gautam Adhikari says in *Times of India* that the
    concept of people evolved over time in USA.
DN: Here politicians ask for overtime allowance.

COBWEB 361

N: An irony please?

DN: In spite of all the progress man has made, he is not able to give life even to a dead fly, but with weapons of mass destruction, he is a mass murderer.

❧

COBWEB 362

N: The dharma of newspapers is that they do not tell all the truth but only the truth when they tell something.

DN: No dharma in the case of paid news.

❧

COBWEB 363

N: Srinivasa Ramanujan solved many problems in maths in his sleep.

DN: I too would have if only I was not disturbed by the sound of my snore.

❧

COBWEB 364

N: Why is a hippopotamus always in water?

DN: It likes to slip.

❧

COBWEB 365

N: One swallow doesn't make a summer.

DN: One sun (star) can blind millions of other stars in the sky.

You may contact the author through
madhuchandini@gmail.com or through 919476584181.